Dear Diary,

Today is my 18th Birthday. I was given this diary as a gift from this man I have been courting. We met at a dance two months ago. He is a private in the army. So dreamy. He is about 6ft tall, very muscular and he has dark hair with the most beautiful blue eyes I have ever seen! All the girls want him but he asked me to dance with him! The girls all stared at us and cut me evil looks. After we danced for a while he walked me home. He kissed me on the cheek and we arranged to meet up again. We met up a few days later, we had a picnic in the park, it was such a lovely day. The sun was shining, the smell of freshly cut grass filled my nostrils. He was so kind, he made me laugh and he was super cute. We had a few more dates and I decided to introduce him to my parents at my birthday party. They liked him. I think it was evident how we felt about each other and they could clearly see how happy he makes me. I think I may be falling in love with him.

He gave me this beautiful diary, he said I can write down my life experiences and one day show them to our children!

Anyway, this is my first entry. After the long yet amazing birthday I have had I need sleep.

Dear Diary,

So it has been a few days since I wrote in this thing! To be truthful I forget I have it. I put it in a safe place and then completely forget that safe place. So I mentioned before that I am courting. His name is Arthur. Arthur Hughes. My tall, dark haired boyfriend! He makes me so happy! Today, he took me shopping and and actually paid for me to have new clothes. He is too kind! My parents still like him. Tomorrow I am invited to Sunday lunch with his family. I feel so nervous! Oops just checked the time! I do not want to look like I am ill from lack of sleep tomorrow. Time to get to sleep!

Dear Diary,

Today I am meeting Arthur's Parents. I have butterflies in my stomach, the thought of eating a whole roast dinner today has my stomach churning. I have already applied my make up and styled my hair with loose curls with my rollers. They are not the best but I don't mind. I decided to wear my white knee length button up dress, it has pink flowers on it so I added my baby pink cardigan and with white flat buckled shoes. Must go! I can hear Arthur downstairs. Here I go!!

Dear Diary,

So today I had dinner with Arthur's parents. Wow! His house is HUGE! Much bigger than my two bedroom town house. He had a huge driveway, gravelled stones as well. The house was massive and had white paint all around the outside walls. The garden was neatly trimmed, regularly cut grass and a variety of flowers. It was beautiful. We don't have grass, just a concrete driveway. Anyway, we were greeted by his parents. They both hugged me and introduced themselves as Patrick and Alice. They were very lovely. Upper class. Unlike me, my family work for minimum wage and we scrape by. The Hughes family don't seem the type to ever want for anything. They have a very comfortable lifestyle. I felt out of place with them. We sat down to eat dinner at a huge dining table, the cloth was pure linen. Very expensive. I had never seen a linen cloth before, we never could afford one. Patrick was at the head of the table as the man of the house, Alice was opposite at the foot of the table. Arthur was sat to Patrick's right and his younger brother William to the left. I was seated next to Arthur, I sure was thankful for that. The conversation was light, his parents wanted to really get to know me, what I liked to eat, read, listen to, my family. After dinner we arranged for them to meet my parents.

Arthur walked me home. He kissed me goodbye on my lips!

I had my first kiss! It was… perfect. I felt everything around us disappear. There was only us in that moment.

Dear Diary,

Tonight Arthur is taking me to a dance. We are going with some of my friends and some of his. William his brother is coming with us as well. I plan on wearing my mint green knee length polka dot dress with green buckle shoes. I am really excited. I love dancing. Arthur and I met at a dance. The sound of a variety of music playing, live singing, a huge dance hall, lots of food and drinks. It is just the best! It is also the only thing we can do for entertainment around here. We live in a small town called Grindley Cove, located in the country side. The nearest town is Fort Delamere and that is an hour away. Arthur and I long for the City. We have discussed relocating one day in the future when we have enough money to make it on our own, rent a place and maybe start a family. I know! We have discussed starting a family! Though a certain question has not been asked! He has promised me an apartment in the City and a little dog. We discussed children. He wants two boys and I don't mind what I have but a boy like him and a girl like me would be perfect. Anyway I am off to this dance!

Dear Diary,

So tonight Arthur and I went dancing with friends. It was a fantastic night! We danced all the way till closing time. When we arrived with William, we spotted our friends at different tables and then we grabbed chairs and became one big group. Arthur introduced me to Frank, Ralph and Leonard. I introduced him to my friends Patty, Delilah, Peggy and Mary. We had a few drinks and some food. Seems our friends were drawn to each other! Mary was asked to dance by Ralph, I did notice how they looked at each other when they were introduced. Then I look over and there is William and Peggy talking rather closely at the drinks bar. Next to us Delilah and Frank were dancing. I smiled at Del. She never was one to date. Or dance. Her two left feet left them tripping over each other. It was rather entertaining. Leonard and Patty were left at the table cuddling together over drinks. The night was pure bliss. The music, the moves. Our friends were getting on better than I ever thought they would. Girls still eyed Arthur from across the room. I know he is attractive, he looks after himself and him and William have inherited their looks from two very attractive parents. The girls gave me dirty looks and made scoffing noises whenever we were near them. Arthur said to ignore them, it is just hard to ignore them when they are acting like that right in front of me, it is not like they were trying to hide how they felt. Anyway I am going to get my dancing feet to bed.

Dear Diary,

There is a town hall meeting tonight. Everyone in town will attend. Nothing serious, it just gives the mayor a chance to mingle and his wife to show herself and her fancy clothes off. They like to do these parties in honour of someone in town. Last party it was to honour the James family. Their sons Marty and Andrew went into business together and upgraded the car sales place. They now have a car wash there and a local shop. Big exciting news. I hate small towns. Anyway I am using this event as a chance to introduce my parents Doris and Larry to Arthur's parents Patrick and Alice. I really hope that they get along. Arthur means so much to me and I know I mean so much to him too.

Dear Diary,

Wow. Tonight. It blew me away. I shall first start with when Arthur picked me up. We drove to the town hall and found a parking space. Luckily, not many people feel the need to drive around here, you can walk to anything, the shops, the school, the library etc... anyway! We met up with my parents and his parents at the entrance. We introduced them and it seemed to be going really well. We headed inside and sat at a table together. The mayor gave his usual speech. But! The family he was honouring was the Hughes family! Arthur and William were asked to accompany Patrick on stage as his sons, they were also following his footsteps and joining the army. They had passed their training together and received a medal for it. So after the applause the mayor announced it was time to eat, drink and be merry. (His words) so that is what we did. Arthur and I went up to the food area together, we both took a tray and piled on food and then collected the drinks before making our way to the table. The conversation was light, our mums talking about how proud they are of us, how lovely we look together and his mum even spoke of wedding bells. Our dads discussed their roles in working and boring male stuff. Ha ha. Then the music started playing and Arthur whisked me over to the floor, leaving our family smiling as they watched us. Patrick and Alice were dancing and I caught my parents swaying together in the corner of my eye. William had left earlier and I saw him at the food area with Peggy, she was giggling and they were touching. The music changed from fast songs, to slow ones, then some country themes came on. The live band were great. From out of town I could tell, the accent was very different. The evening was in full swing. I danced with my dad and even Patrick asked me for a dance. Arthur danced with his mum and my mum. Everyone got along so well. I really could not be happier than in that moment. I then sat at the table, thirsty from all the dancing. I was having a drink and picking at the food on my plate when the mayor's voice came through the microphone. He said that Arthur wanted to make an announcement. At first I thought I misheard him, but Arthur was making his way on the stage up the steps. My mouth sure hung open in that moment. Arthur spoke into the microphone about how he was grateful that everyone came out tonight and celebrated his and William's training success, he went on to thanking the town for the medals and how honoured he was feeling. I look around the table, his parents are smiling with pride and my mum is smiling too. But my dad was looking at me. Then Arthur jumps down off the stage, microphone in hand!! I could not believe it! He was walking towards me, holding his microphone, he lead me to the middle of the floor. The whole town was watching from their tables. The mayor and his wife smiling at us with pride. I had no idea what was going on. Then! He got down on one knee. Looking up at me from the floor, he told me how his life had become the best he could ask for since meeting me, he told the whole town how happy I made him, how much he loved me and how much a future with me is all he wants. He did however leave out our plans to relocate to the city. Then he took out this small black box, I could feel my knees shaking in that moment. I had butterflies and I swear I nearly vomited.

Then he lifted the lid and inside, was a ring so beautiful and shiny I thought it would make me blind. The ring was white gold, with a sapphire centre diamond with crystals around the edges. It was beautiful. Taking the ring from the box he stood up to his full height, placing it on the tip of my finger he asked me to marry him! I could feel my face splitting I was smiling so widely. Of course I said yes! He was the love of my life. After I said yes, he slipped the ring down my finger and we kissed. I forgot the whole town was watching until I heard them all clapping. Stopping for air we turned to our friends and family, with huge grins on our faces. My mum came to see the ring and his parents hugged me and welcomed me to the family. The mayor got back on stage and said his congratulations and then everyone was back to eating, drinking and dancing. Arthur and I stayed with our family at the table and we drank and ate and celebrated our news together. After the dance, the towns people congratulated us when we were leaving the town hall. I climbed into his car and we kissed some more. Then he drove me home. I have been on cloud nine ever since. I am tired, happy, excited so many different emotions. I want to sleep but I needed to write this down. Arthur gave me this precious diary to record my memories and experiences. This one is one of many that I never want to forget. I really cannot wait to share this with my children. One day.

Dear Diary,
So today Arthur and I are planning to go to the next town, they are having a spring fair and we want to spend the day together. I am definitely looking forward to leaving this town for a day. The people are all the same and I want to see more. Arthur is here now.

Dear Diary,

So we left town for a few hours and we went to Fort Delamere. It was a nice change of scenery. The town was quite similar to ours, local shops, a school and a few houses scattered around the outside. The town hall in the middle of the town. The only difference, is that we have a church. The same church Arthur and I plan to marry in next month. Yes! At the fair we set a date. We had look around the stalls, played a few games and rode on the Ferris wheel. That was scary! Heights are not for me I realised today. Arthur treated me to lunch from the hot dog stand and even won me a teddy bear. It was a lovely day. We strolled along, hand in hand, talked about our future and we told each other how much we loved each other. We even named our children!! Arthur wants two boys. Ray and John. I want a boy called John and I would love a daughter, I would name her Alice. Such a beautiful name and his mum is called Alice. He drove me home and kissed me goodbye on my doorstep. We have arranged to meet up at the next dance in a few days. Our parents have a surprise for us. An engagement surprise. I am excited to see what they have for us!

Dear Diary,

So tonight is the night of the dance. Arthur has arranged to pick me up later tonight, but we are seeing each other in a few hours because our parents want to give us our gift. Arthur is picking me and my parents up and we are meeting at Patrick and Alice's house. I am feeling really nervous yet excited. I am insecure about my parents seeing the Hughes household, it is much, much larger than ours and they clearly have a lot more money than us. I don't want my parents feeling inferior and out of place like I did when I first went there. They were so down to earth and so kind and warm and welcoming I couldn't help but relax. I only hope my parents feel the same way.

Dear Diary,

Arthur has just dropped me and my parents home. We had
a lovely time. We met at his parent's home and my parents
actually relaxed. They didn't seem fazed by the money or
the big house, Alice was her usual warm and welcoming self
and Patrick and my dad just hit it off again, talking boring
man things. We sat down to lunch at the dining table, I
was seated next to Arthur again which again I was very
happy about. We ate and the conversation flowed, no
silences. William and Peggy were there as well, that was
nice. It was a very relaxing time. After lunch we gathered
in the lounge and had some home made cake from Alice,
the sponge was so fluffy, the jam and cream so sweet and
then the icing on top made it completely perfect. I felt
very naught asking for an extra slice but Alice was more
than happy to cut me one. After some sweet tea we had
conversation at the dining table again and that is when
Arthur and I received our gift. Our parents said they all
arranged it and thought it would be perfect for us. They
all actually paid for us to have a night away in the City of
Maybird for our wedding night! Can you believe it! Our
wedding night is planned and our wedding date set, all that
is left to do is meet with the vicar in Fort Delamere and
send out invitations. Arthur said I can have any dress I
want and Alice and my mum are coming with me dress
hunting this Saturday! Everything is falling into place.

Dear Diary,

So Arthur came back tonight and we went to dance. The girls met us there and the guys soon followed, everyone had a dance partner. We had our own table and ordered drinks and some food. We casually talked and had a really good time. Arthur and I would dance to the slow songs and I would dance to the fast songs with my girls while the guys looked on. Oh my god. You will not believe it, there was some HUGE drama tonight!! A guy, unknown to us approached Mary! He is from out of town by the way he dressed and his accent. He approached her at the bar while she was ordering drinks. He started talking to her and quickly put his hands on her! Well that sent Ralph into a frenzy. He approached the man and told him to take his hands off his woman, all the guys in our group of friends went to Ralph's side when the other guy now known as Freddie called his mates over to his side. Once the new guys realised all the girl's in this group were taken they moved on to other side of the room and we continued to ear, drink and dance. Arthur drove me home, tomorrow I have plans with our mothers but later tomorrow night he is staying in with his brother and dad so I am using that time to spend with my girls. We are having a sleepover at Mary's house while her parents are out of town on business. We kissed goodbye and I spent the evening with my parents and the radio.

Dear Diary,

Today I am heading into town with my mum and Alice. We are going for lunch at the local café and then going to the local bridal shop. I hope I find something other wise we will have to get the bus into the next town and I don't feel up for that today. I have been looking in the window when I have passed the shop and some have caught my eye. So here is hoping I can pick one. I know what style I have in my mind, just hoping I can find one at a reasonable price. My dad is paying for it and I know the money he has given my mum has taken us back a bit for this month, hope it is worth it. If I can help it, I try not to ask them for money. I pay my way from doing the odd jobs but I know they still struggle. Well Alice is here now so here I go.

Dear Diary,

Well I found my dress!!! It is beautiful. Cream silk material. Knee length plead skirt. Absolutely lovely. It was more in price than my father gave my mother. I was really embarrassed and even offered to try on a sale dress but Alice wouldn't hear of it. She took my mum over to the side as I stared at them through the mirror in the dress, the beautiful dress. I am not sure what Alice said, they were talking in hushed voices. My mum seemed to eagerly agree with her, no hesitation what so ever. They then approached me and said I could have the dress! We then went to have something to eat and drink. It was lovely. I am now back home after hanging up my dress and changing into my plead full length grey skirt and short sleeve white top. I decided to wear black buckle shoes. My hair is in a bun on my head and I am off to meet my friends.

Dear Diary,

So last night after wedding dress shopping I had some well earned girl time. We slept over at Mary's house. We had snacks and Peggy snuck in some naughty drinks from her father. We had blankets and cushions on the floor around Mary's bed and we had the radio on. We talked fashion, boys and my wedding. Everyone was excited to be my maids. They all had picked their favourite dresses they owned. We got talking about boys again and Peggy asked who had gone further than kissing with the boys and they all said yes! I had actually felt my cheeks flush. I thought you didn't do stuff like that until you were married. I felt awkward because they were my friends and I knew the guys well. They all told of their experiences, some were pretty bad but got better the more they did it, some it was okay and just gets better some were good and stayed average. They all then turned to me! I was so flustered! I actually admitted that me and Arthur had never gone further than kissing, I had never been in his bedroom and he certainly would not be allowed in mine!! None of my friends judged me. They said what we had was special and that the wedding night will be the night. That made me feel really nervous. I love Arthur, completely and I want marriage and a family with him in the City but am I really ready to be naked in front of him, let him see me like that, touch me like that and even be intimate? Panic filled me for the rest of the night. We laughed, drank and snacked on foods but it was still at the back of my mind. Was I ready?

Dear Diary,

Today Arthur is going to get his wedding clothes with his dad. My dad asked to tag along and Patrick was delighted to have the company. I am still so happy that our parents get on. Unlike some of our friend's parents. Delilah's mum didn't like Frank's dad, she thought him too full on and well there had been some arguments between them over family members. Arthur and I are very lucky. Tonight when I see him later, I am going to ask him how he feels about intimacy, what my friends have said and how insecure I feel about it all. I don't want to be pressured into this but I am interested to see what Arthur thinks about it. We have never discussed it before, we have talked about children yes, but not how we make them!! I know what you do to make them but we always said children after marriage and well these days you are proper if you marry first. It is how it is done. However like my friends there are a few towns people who did not wait until marriage. The family that live next door to me, well Mrs Wayne, she first dated the local mechanic Marty Hall. They had a relationship in high school and she became pregnant with her son Frederick. They did not last. They spilt up after he was born, a few years later she married Mr Wayne. Marty married Dorris Junes. I know Marty sees Frederick, but that is an example of someone who had sex before marriage and it didn't end in a wedding. I do not want that for me and Arthur. I want us to last forever. I love him so much. We have so many wonderful plans together. The perfect life.

Dear Diary,

So Arthur found his suit. My dad told me when he got back. He told me how Patrick, William and Arthur were fitted and my dad said they all looked very smart. My dad will buy his wedding outfit another time. He is not shopping at that suit shop, too expensive for us. He will travel to Fort Delamere later this week. Tonight I am meeting up with Arthur, he has planned a romantic date. A complete surprise. I have no idea where we are going, what we are doing or what kind of outfit I should wear. Well I have just settled with my polka dot knee length skirt and a top. Will take a cardigan in case it cools down. I have left my hair in a high pony tail and no make up. I barely wear it. It is very expensive. Well I am heading out now, to my surprise date with my Arthur.

Dear Diary,

So tonight Arthur took me to the woods not far from here. We parked the car up and walked hand in hand. He lay out a blanket and he had brought snacks and drinks. The air was chilly and Arthur gave me his jacket. We lay down after we ate and drank. Looking up at the night sky. A navy colour with bright stars. Beautiful. We held hands and kissed. Arthur gave me a new name. He called me Mags. Ha. It will take me a while to get used to Mags. People call me Maggie and when I am in trouble with my parents I hear Maggie - Leigh!! Ha. Between holding hands while kissing and gazing up to the stars I managed to talk to him about intimacy, what my friends said and how I felt about it. Well he sure did reassure me that he would not pressure me. He said he wants to wait until we are married, he said it will be special and we can be close as husband and wife, as it should be. My heart became more full for him. In a few more weeks we will be married. We meet the vicar tomorrow. We are heading to Fort Delamere first thing in the morning to meet him after his first service before his afternoon one. I am so excited. I am ready to be Mrs Maggie - Leigh Hughes.

Dear Diary,

I have on my Sunday best. My straight knee length black skirt and black blouse with white polka dots on with black buckle shoes. I have curled my hair and left my face clear. I am so nervous. Soon I will be stood in front of a vicar, declaring my love for Arthur and praying he gives us his blessing to marry. If we get the yes we so desperately want, we will be shown around the church and we get to pick flower arrangements and seating. Also we will meet the congregation that will too witness our wedding as well as our family and friends. Well Arthur is here now and we have a long drive ahead of us.

Dear Diary,

So Arthur and I met with the vicar today. We got a YES! Ha! We are so happy. We met with the congregation, we picked out some flowers and arranged the seating for the family, the bride side and the groom side. The church is so big and beautiful. We marry there in two weeks time. On the drive back, he held my hand and kissed it. We were so happy. When he dropped me off at home, my parents invited him in and we had sweet tea while we talked about the church and the arrangement. My mum hand – made the guest invitations. They are beautiful. They will be sent out today now we have a date. Two weeks today. So much to do so little time. I saw Arthur out, I stood on the door step and we kissed goodbye, I get to see him tonight as we are spending time with friends.

Dear Diary,

So tonight, Arthur picked me up and we walked over to Peggy's house. Her parents are staying with her grandparents in the next town. We played card games, ate snacks and drank. We danced to the radio. It was so much fun. Arthur and I kept leaving to stand in the back garden to have privacy while we kissed and held hands. We are so in love. In two weeks time we become husband and wife. I get to spend the rest of my life with the man I love. He has my heart completely. He is my soul mate. My partner for life and my very best friend.

Dear Diary,

I am heading into the next town today, I promised my mum I would help her choose her outfit for the wedding. It is now in three days time! The invites were sent out. Our friends and family will all be joining us. Arthur and I are delighted! It will be perfect. The mayor agreed that we could have the town hall, for the after party so that the towns people could get a chance to celebrate with us as only family and the congregation will be in the church.

Dear Diary,

Well mum and I headed into the next town. She found a very nice knee length skirt and a red blouse. She will look lovely. Tonight I am seeing Peggy and Delilah. Were are meeting up because these two want ideas for their hair. Everyone else is all ready.

Dear Diary,

My wedding day. I could vomit. Butterflies are swirling around in my stomach. I have Alice's curlers in my hair. They are much more expensive than mine and will certainly give me curls unlike mine. She has applied my light make up and I am being fitted into my dress. My friends are changing in the room as well. There are hair accessories and clothes all over the room. We are using Alice's house to change in. All the men are changing at my house. They will be heading to the church before us. We hired a couple of cars to take all the guests. The congregation will already be there. In two cars, there will be Patrick, William, Arthur, Frank and Ralph in one car. Larry will follow behind with Leonard. We also have two cars. One will have me, my dad and my mum, with Peggy and Mary. The other one will have Delilah and Alice in. my dad is walking me down the isle and he is tearing up already. Well the cars are here for us. Here I go.

Dear Diary,

I am officially Mrs Arthur Hughes. The wedding ceremony was lovely. My dad walked me down the isle, Arthur and I said our vows and then we had congratulations and confetti thrown over us as we left the church. Everyone got back in the cars and we headed to the town hall. The mayor and his wife we waiting for us at the doors. They congratulated us and we were walked into the main room where the whole town waited for us while being seated at tables. Arthur and I had the main table where the Mayor and his wife usually sat. They sat with their children to the right of us on a separate table. Everyone danced, ate and got merry. Arthur and I had our first dance. I danced with my dad and Patrick. We were then walked outside where a car was waiting for us to take us on the three hour journey to the City of Maybird to stay there for tonight. We got in the car and our cases were already in the boot. The driver had the directions and we waved our family, friends and neighbours goodbye. I fell asleep in the car and was woken up when we were outside of the hotel. Arthur helped me out of the car and we signed in. Our room is lovely. There is a double bed, wardrobe and a radio. They even shown us where the shared bathroom is. It is located two doors down the hall on the left hand side. I had to bring this diary with me. I had to write down about my wedding night. Well Arthur is turning the radio off. My guess is it is time to go to bed.

Dear Diary,

Wow. My wedding night. Arthur watched me as I put my diary back in my case. He said he was glad I was using it. I never told him how much I have used it but he knows I like to write in it. So we got changed into our nightwear and settled into bed! Together! We kissed and then we started to undress each other. It was very fast. Our hands shaking, we were fumbling around with each others clothes. We both giggled so much. I could tell I wasn't the only one who was nervous. I felt so vulnerable being alone with him, naked and exposed. He was so gentle. It was a very nice experience. One I was happy to have shared with my Arthur. I think we liked it a little too much. We couldn't keep our hands off each other last night and we ended up being intimate a few more times before we fell asleep in each others arms. Well today, we are planning to see the City, look at apartments before we return to Grindley Cove.

Dear Diary,

We are back at the hotel room. Just finished packing our things up, the driver will be back in an hour or so. Our time in the City was amazing. It is so BIG! We went into a few shops, memorised road names and then we went to see about apartments and renting. It was not easy. Some agents were very hard to deal with. But! We did find a very nice lady agent and she shown us some apartments and we even viewed one. We put down our details and Arthur paid money up front. We explained that we had to tell our family before we move in and she was very understanding. I started to feel a lump form in my throat. I was so concentrated on the wedding and living with Arthur that I forgot that I will be leaving my family behind me. With there being three hours between us I doubt I will see them as often as I would like. The driver is here. Tonight we head home. Tomorrow we meet with all our parents together.

Dear Diary,

Well today Arthur and I are meeting at his parent's house. We are planning to tell all our parents together that we have plans to move to the City, we have an apartment lined up and I will search for work when we get settled. I really do not know how they will all take this news.

Dear Diary,

Well our moving to the city news went very... WELL!! our family were very supportive of our decisions. They all teared up yes, but they all just wanted us to be safe. William seemed cut up about it, losing his only brother to the City, unsure on what to do when the time came for them to go to war. If it ever came. That time is one we hope never to come knocking on our door.

Dear Diary,

Today we say goodbye to our parents. Our cases are packed, Alice and Patrick gave us some money for furniture and decorations for the house. My parents gave us second hand kitchen essentials. It will be a very sad day. Today I say goodbye to my family and friends. I also say goodbye to the town I was born and raised in. But! Today I also start a new life with the man I love in a City.

Dear Diary,

There was not a dry eye in Grindley Cove today. Our family and friends gave a teary farewell. Our neighbours, the towns people and the Mayor also came to wave us off. I cried the whole journey to the City. We got the key and we settled our cases and the few boxes we had in the lounge area. We had already had a mattress delivered here a few days ago so we had somewhere to sleep. This is my new home. My home with Arthur. Our new life begins now. We are planning on settling in, making this place a home and then I will look for a small job to add money to the pot while we plan our little family.

Dear Diary,

Well a week into our new life, we got ourselves into a steady routine. Today after I got home from grocery shopping and Arthur surprised me with a huge box with holes in. It was placed on our new sofa. Duck egg sofa. I decided duck egg and yellow in my lounge. My lounge. Anyway I open the lid and inside is a little puppy. He was so cute, he jumped straight into my arms. We named him Bruno. Arthur told me some brilliant news too. Our parents were coming to visit soon, now that we had some rooms decorated and we were settling in fine, they all wanted to come see our home. I am delighted!

Dear Diary,

It has been three whole months since I wrote in this. I keep it locked in a draw by the side of my bed. Well these last few months have been HECTIC! Our parents come to see us quite often and we are planning a trip to see them. Only the trip is not a very good one. Arthur and William have been called up. Some battle has broke out between our country and somewhere else. I am devastated. I don't want him to leave. I am scared for him. For him and William. Of course with Patrick being the leader he must leave too. I feel sorry for Peggy and Alice, Peggy unfortunately became pregnant. Her and William are not yet married and if he is killed, the child will be unclaimed and a bastard. Luckily, Alice and Patrick have given him their word that they will look after Peggy and the child. Arthur and I have been unfortunate in the family area. We are trying but it does not happen. Every month we are disappointed. I know Arthur is so supportive but I can see each time it destroys a small part of him. The fear of never giving him a child eats away at me everyday. He so desperately wants a son and I really want a child of his growing inside me too. I want it so much I long for it.

Dear Diary,

I am staying with Patrick and Alice tonight. Arthur and William left today. I cried so hard into his chest as he held me tight. He promised me a safe return and I believed him. Patrick even said it was a minor battle and will probably be sorted within a few weeks. It eased my fears a little. At dinner, Alice said Patrick will take me back to my home tomorrow. Mine and Arthur's home. I came to bed not long after supper. I really could not eat much tonight and I just wanted to go to bed. I am missing Arthur so much! I miss cuddling with him before we went to sleep. I miss his smell and the way he kisses my forehead before sleep consumes me. Instead tonight I am lying in his old bed, in his old room, in his parent's house without him. His smell burning my nostrils and leaving a huge ache in my heart.

Dear Diary,

I have been home for over two weeks now. Arthur is still away and Patrick joined them a week ago. Arthur writes to me when he can. His letters give me hope. He is still with me. He sends his love, tells me about his day, how he is getting extra training, how much he misses me and our dog. He tells me how William writes to Peggy. I am yet to write back. I am eager, very eager to tell him our news. I went to the doctor today, feeling unwell. I found out I am with child. We finally did it. We are having a child together. We are going to be a family.

Dear Diary,

I never heard from Arthur again. I have been asked to go back to Grindley Cove. A car is picking me up in a few moments. I have packed a case for a few days and will be taking Bruno with me. I am yet to tell our families our news. I am hoping to see Arthur today. I am hoping to that this is one big surprise. That the reason Arthur never sent another letter again was because he wanted to surprise me when he came home. I am a little confused why he didn't return to Maybird but he must want to see his mum.

Dear Diary,

Tonight I arrived at Patrick and Alice's house. My parents were there. Everyone had red eyes and Alice was out of control sobbing. I didn't understand. Where was my Arthur. I soon found out. Tonight William took me to the side of the dining room and told me news I never wanted to receive. He told me my Arthur was dead. Gone. He gave me his hat and his medals and the one last letter he never had chance to send. They then told me the funeral will be held here TOMORROW! Can you believe it? I am burying my husband tomorrow. While I have his child growing inside me, I bury him. The child he will never know, or see or feel.

Dear Diary,

The funeral took place in the church in Fort Delamere. The same church we married in only a few months ago. It was awful. I just stared at the coffin. Not believing all of this. It must be a mistake. The wrong Arthur. No. He was in there. My husband. The father of my child. The love of my life. After the funeral I returned home. Here I am in our home, working out how I am going to afford this place, my dog and my baby on the way. I never got a chance to tell my family or his family about our arrival. It did not seem right. How silly. The perfect time to tell his parents that they will have a grandson from Arthur and I. Yet I just returned home. To our home. I wanted to feel him again, be near him again. I have a doctors appointment in a week, he won't be there with me. When I deliver this baby he won't be there with me either.

Dear Diary,

Doctors appointments have come and gone. I finally told our families and my parents actually came with me to the last one. Alice and Patrick have helped me with baby supplies. I am working a little job, I can have maternity leave and then return to work. It also pays my rent and bills and I am able to live comfortably with a baby and Bruno. Our families have been so kind. So welcoming of our young child. Our baby. Today I am heading to work and then doing the grocerie shopping afterwards. I have a midwife, she comes to see me nightly, in case I go into labour. I have no idea what my beautiful baby looks like or if it is a boy or a girl. I have names. Arthur and I chose John for a boy and I secretly chose Alice for a girl. I can feel it kicking. My back aches and my ankles are swollen. Off to work I go.

Dear Diary,

Today started off okay, I finished tidying up and then my stomach started cramping. I am now resting in bed with Bruno, the cramping is still happening and I am waiting for my midwife to arrive so I can tell her. I am sweaty and hot, my back is hurting, the cramping harder, faster.

Dear Diary,

So it has been almost two weeks since I wrote in this. I had my beautiful baby delivered by my midwife two weeks ago today. I was laying in bed and the midwife pushed open the front door when she heard me screaming for her after I heard the ringing. I was so glad she was there. I told her everything, the cramping the pains, the burning pain at the time she walked in. my baby's head was crowning. My beautiful baby was on their way into the world. I pushed and I panted for what felt like forever and then I heard the tiny cry. The cutest tiniest cry I ever did hear! My beautiful daughter Alice was born. She was born with jet black hair and beautiful piercing blue eyes. She looked just like her father. My Arthur would have been proud of me. He would of loved meeting our daughter. Patrick and Alice travelled to see us and they even surprised me by bringing my parents. They stayed in a hotel together for a week, we did some sight seeing in the City, I showed them where I worked, the local park I will be taking Bruno and now Alice too. Alice loved her granddaughters name! They all told me how proud they were of me. How proud Arthur would be if he was here. For the past week, it has just been me, Alice and Bruno, we are getting into a nice routine. I have found a child carer. She worked as a midwife, had her children, fostered a few more and then became a carer for children. She was perfect. She has Alice while I work. I pay her monthly with my earnings.

Dear Diary,

Alice is now four weeks old. She is doing really well. The doctors are happy with her growth, she seems to love Bruno and his big nose and has taken a likening to the child minder, Mrs Marthwells. Bruno is great with Alice, he is gentle around her, no longer a puppy he is really boisterous. I found another job, I now work as a cleaner in the morning and a waitress in the afternoon. Both jobs leave me and Alice with a comfortable life. Arthur would be proud of me. Because I work so many hours in the day I am sure to give my darling Alice my full attention at night.

Dear Diary,

Alice is now six months old. Alice and Patrick come to visit us regularly. This weekend I plan to show Alice my home town. William and Peggy are expecting their second child and I am eager to meet their son James. I am packing our cases today so that they are ready. Alice needs so much in just one day, for an entire weekend I shall need a few cases. I am being picked up by Patrick's driver. I am also taking my precious Bruno with me.

Dear Diary,

This weekend was lovely. I got to see my friends, all of which are mothers and mums to be. I got to see my family and I also saw my in laws. It was perfect. I saw a few towns people that I thought I never would again, some are grey and ageing.

Dear Diary,

Six months have passed, I have been so busy raising Alice, I forget to write in this. Today was her first birthday. Everyone came to our home, all our family and friends. They brought presents and cards, I even had a cake made for her. The only downside, Bruno was not his usual self, his breathing uneasy and shallow. I have to get him checked out tomorrow by a special doctor who specialises in animals tomorrow.

Dear Diary,

Today I had to let the animal doctor kill my Bruno. He injected him. Said he had something wrong with his lungs and that it would be unkind to keep him alive. I cried while I held my darling dog in my arms. I held him and rocked him while he slowly closed his eyes. I felt him take his last breath as a tear slid down my cheek and dropped onto his nose. Afterwards I went to the child minder and took Alice in my hands, I kissed her and hugged and carried her all the way home. I gave her some tea and told her I loved her very much. I bathed her and read her a story in bed. Once she closed her eyes I kissed her cheek. Now I am lying in my bed. No Arthur. No Bruno. Just me.

Dear Diary,

Today I have my parents coming over to visit. I have dressed Alice and set the table for lunch. I am excited to see them, I don't get to see them too often and Alice misses them dearly. Well I am yet to dress myself, I chose my knee length button down red dress with white polka dots. Best go finish off getting ready.

Dear Diary,

So my parents came this afternoon. I told them about poor Bruno, they brought a new dress for Alice and some china cups for me. Very fancy. I knew it must of set them back. Sometimes I feel guilty for living such a comfortable life in the City while they are stuck in that small town trying to get by, living each day as it comes. Not knowing when they can pay this bill or that bill or even eat. I take all the gifts they give me yes but I still feel the money they spend on them could go towards their own lives. We sat down at my new dining table, I cooked some soup, we then ate some rice and meat, then I served up some nice cake, the child minder kindly baked for me. The conversation flowed nicely and we hugged for a while longer than normally as they were leaving. They kissed Alice goodbye and I am hoping to travel there as soon as I can some time off work. I have two jobs so I work different times and I am given different holidays for each, it's hard finding a date that I have off for both jobs.

Dear Diary,

Tonight Alice and I sat down to tea, we had news from
Alice and Patrick were coming to visit us in a weeks time,
Alice was very excited to see them. She looks more and
more like Arthur everyday. Her dark is hair is getting
longer and her blue eyes are getting brighter. She really is
his double. Sometimes the things she says or does remind
me so much of her father. He would be so proud of her.
He would have fallen in love with her immediately. I know he
wanted boys but I know one look into those eyes would
have had him hooked. I know I am. I do spoil her a little
too much as well. She has her own room and I decorated it
how she wanted it. She chose the paint, she wanted yellow.
She wanted one wall to have white polka dots and I did
that for her. I can afford to give her good sheets and
bedding and her draws are full of lovely clothes. She has
toys in there. I guess I am trying to give her a childhood
I never had. There is colour in her room, toys all around,
teddies fill a hanging net on one wall. I just want her
happy. While I have two jobs we can afford the life we
live. The nice City apartment, the nice clothes, the toys
for Alice. We eat better than I ever did and my cooking
skills are getting better each day. As much as I work I
always make sure I leave cooked food for Alice to have
every night before she sleeps. Warm her belly up and help
her sleep on a full stomach. I remember the agony of
trying to sleep while your stomach is cramping and rumbling.
Sometimes I would only go to bed on a slice of bread. It
was not enough. I make sure Alice has a heavy cooked meal
to fill her up. I leave breakfast and lunch instructions. Now

that Alice turned one I have her enrolled at a local nursery for this coming fall. I will no longer need the child minder full time, just in the evenings as I work then as well. Weekends I spend with Alice, we go to the park, I have taken her to see a few shows, we even have picnics on our lounge floor while listening to the radio sometimes. Well after today I am ready to get some sleep. Back to work tomorrow for me.

Dear Diary,

I work so hard cleaning. That job sure does take my energy. The smell of cleaning products burning my nose is unbearable. But well I need the money if me and Alice are going to continue to live this nice life. Later I am due to wait tables and after that I am going to grab a bath and head to bed.

Dear Diary,

Home finally after waiting those tables. Some of the men that come in there are vile animals. They think they can touch you inappropriately and say vile things to you. I have to grin and bear it if I want to keep my job. I really hate working with those vile men being in there. I do have friends though, my boss is great, I get along with all the waitresses, most of them are single mothers too. Lost their husbands in the battle. Like me. The chef is great too. I really do enjoy eating his food, he makes us all a plateful after closing hours and we eat, laugh and I drink juice not alcohol. It's a very relaxed work place. I am not alone like I am when I am cleaning. Well I am going to jump in a hot bubble bath and get some sleep.

Dear Diary,

This long week at work went so slow. Finally the weekend is here and I am waiting for Alice and Patrick to arrive. I have set everything out, Alice is wearing her new dress my parents brought for her. I am wearing basic clothing today. To be honest, I usually dread their visits. They like to point out flaws in my decorating or flaws in the way I am raising Alice. I love them too bits but they really have changed, when I first met them they were so kind, warm and welcoming, really down to earth. Now they are always pointing out bad points or complaining about how Alice is. Well the car has just arrived. Best go put on my famous hostess smile.

Dear Diary,

Well today went as well as expected. Alice picked out flaws in my wallpaper. Said I need to decorate more often than I do. It was fresh up that month. Then she complained my food was cold, or the bread too hard. Patrick complained that Alice needed a bigger room and we needed a house with a garden. Not a tiny flat (his words) I am just so annoyed. Then after we ate, we sat down to some sweet tea and cake. They both said that Alice seems unwell, said her cough was not normal and she looked pale. I only noticed she had a cough when they mentioned it, usually when Alice feels unwell she asks for a hot water bottle and more soup. Now I know Alice does seem to have a rather nasty cough I shall get the local doctor round to see her first thing tomorrow. Well now they have finally gone, I am going to make a flask of soups and warm up a bottle for Alice before she goes to bed.

Dear Diary,

The doctor is coming round in a couple of hours. When I told him of her cough he asked if she had a high temperature, she didn't at that time. She was however very pale. I have kept her in her pyjamas and left her in bed. She said she doesn't want to get up this morning. Very unlike my bouncy, lively Alice.

Dear Diary,

The doctor has just left. He said she has some kind of flu and to keep her warm, plenty of food and fluids and to keep him updated should she get worse. My poor baby girl has the flu. I really do not know how she got it. She is never allowed out if it rains and she always wears a coat and gloves in the cold air. I am so scared right now.

Dear Diary,

I gave Alice her lunch soup and made sure she was warm and comfortable. She has a radio for company and I can hear her should she shout for me. I had to take time off work as the doctor said she might get worse and will need me not a child minder. My jobs did not seem to mind, I am even being paid for my absence on the basic of sick from my waitress job. I was listening to my own radio whilst ironing clothes in my bedroom when a certain news broadcast came on. Apparently people in towns and Cities were falling ill with some kind of flu and most if not all cases resulted in death. More and more children were dying from this flu as they were not as strong to fight it as a fully grown adult. I felt my knees go weak. What if my Alice had this flu? Would she be strong enough to fight against it? I can't lose my only tie to Arthur, my beloved Alice, she is my life, my whole reason for living. With out her I am nothing.

Dear Diary,

I had to call the doctor again. Alice got worse in the night, coughing up blood and have nose bleeds after sneezing. She has gone off food completely and wont drink anything either. I have got water by her bed and I regularly heat up her water bottle. The doctor said there is nothing he can do. We just have to keep Alice comfortable and wait to see if she can fight it. I had to leave the cleaning job as they said they needed to hire someone else because I was the only cleaner doing that location. I was devastated. My boss at the restaurant said I can keep my job as long as I do an evening a week and can still have full pay, I just need to show my face. I have arranged for the child minder to come twice a week so that I can still work. I will write down my instructions for her with Alice as well. Thankfully the child minder does not mind that Alice is poorly and could possibly contagious. So far I have no symptoms and have been checked over by the doctor and was given the green light to go to work an evening or two once a week. I really could not turn down the offer to have full pay and only work two evenings, I have bills and Alice will have medical bills at the end of the month. I am not sure how much they will cost. The doctor said it could be quite a lot as he is coming to the house, taking him away from his other patients at the surgery. Even though he has not given her any medication. There is nothing he can do he says. I am beside myself. I really cannot lose my Alice. I cant face the fact that she might not fight this, I have to stay calm and have faith that she will fight this flu and everything will be all right. I pray every day.

Dear Diary,

I have been working two evenings a week for the past three weeks. Alice is not getting any better. The doctor wants his first payment soon and I am working as hard as I can for it. My rent is due tomorrow and I have my bill money coming out soon as well. Alice is decreasing fast, she no longer eats, she can no longer move. She lies in bed all day, we have to move her because her skin has become scabby and sore. We bath her everyday, he hair becoming dry, her skin becoming tight, she looks skeletal. Her rosy cheeks no longer pink, just white, her bright blue eyes are dull. She no longer smiles. She is slowly dying. There has been no sign of her body fighting this. I cannot and will not come to terms with losing my baby. She can fight this. I talk to her all the time. Tell her how beautiful she is, how strong she is. How young she is and how she is going to fight this illness.

Dear Diary,

Alice took a turn for the worse today. I was at work. When I got home, the doctor was there with the child minder. He said that she had been vomiting and that her breathing was shallow. He took me into my room, while the child minder held Alice's hand. He told me that it was possible Alice might not make the night. He said that I should be prepared. Be prepared! How can I? My baby girl is slowly dying and I can't stand the thought of losing her. I won't let her go. She really cannot leave me! I won't let her.

Dear Diary,

Alice died at 10:10pm. I held her hand and kissed her forehead when she took her last breath. I cried so much, the doctor gave me something to help me sleep. Tomorrow I am to meet the doctor at the surgery. He wants to go through the next procedure. I am hoping to take Alice back to my home town. I will bury her there. I want to stay with my parents and have them hold my hand. Comfort me. My life is over. My daughter is gone. My dog Bruno is gone. My beloved Arthur is gone. I am all alone. She came into my life when I needed her the most and now she is gone.

Dear Diary,

Today is the day of the funeral. We are in Fort Delamere.
She is being buried next to her father. When I arrived
home, my parents held me all night while I cried. Alice and
Patrick have been so comforting. Helping with the funeral
arrangements and even taking on some of the payments for
it. Today I bury my one year old child in the same grave
as her father.

Dear Diary,

Alice has been gone for two months. I left my waitress job, gave up my apartment and started living with my parents again. My friends come to see me everyday if they can, they have their own children to look after. William is brilliant. He brings me food and gifts from him and Peggy. I have started working at the local shop behind the till. The wage is no where near what I was on but it is enough to pay my parents housekeeping and enough to buy flowers for Alice and Arthur every week. I have nightmares at night. I scream for my Alice. She can't be gone. I won't except it. My mum comes in every night with warm cocoa and comforts me.

Dear Diary,

I haven't wrote in this thing much. I have been spending the last six months coming to terms with the loss of my Alice. I have been working hard and looking for my own place. I came across an arrogant out of town gentleman today. Thinking he could sweet talk me, the money he checked in was a lot so he must be rich. He had fine clothing and his hair was well looked after. I got the impression that he was used to getting his own way. He did not seem to like my rejection. I told him I was a happily married mother and he needs to look else where. Anyway I am off to work again, my shift patterns are different each day.

Dear Diary,

So the arrogant gentleman came back. Taking out even more money. Seems he did his research on me. Told me I was a widow with a child in the ground. It cut me deep. The way he said it. It sent a chill down my spine. Like he liked the thought I was available for the taking. He will never take me. My heart and body belong to my Arthur and the only child I want is my Alice.

Dear Diary,

The mayor is having an event in the town hall tonight. To celebrate the town. I remember his events so well. The last one I attended was to congratulate Arthur and William with their army training. Remembering it brings tears to my eyes. I wish I could have Arthur hold me now. Tell me everything is going to be okay. He would keep that vile man in line and he would never bother me again.

Dear Diary,

I went to the event with my parents. The Mayor welcomed the vile man now known as Bernard. Apparently he is rich man from the City of Wallow Pine. Apparently he wants to invest money into this town. Bring it up to date like the other towns and even help with expanding it. I was at a table with my parents. Bernard was making conversation with Alice and Patrick and every now and then they would all look my way. My parents would look away and my dad would try to take my mind off it. Alice and Patrick never looked my way again after Bernard walked away from them. I have no idea what they were discussing. As the parents of my husband surely they would not allow me to be taken by that vile man. I am the mother of their granddaughter.

Well, I was their son's wife. I was the mother of their granddaughter. Now I am nothing to them. With both my loves lying in the ground I am vulnerable to be taken by vile gentleman like Bernard. I sure will put up a good fight! My mum and dad have promised they will never ever let anything bad happen to me again. I believe them. They say I have been through more than most girls my age and now I am back with them they will fight whoever and whatever to protect me.

But we all know, they are tiny, nothing townspeople next to big rich outsiders. I only hope that he will leave soon.

Dear Diary,

Bernard has been snooping around my home. My dad told him where to stick his money and to leave us alone. The Mayor has been involved in my mum's harassment case against Bernard. All he cares about is Bernard's money and what it will do for his town. No one in this town cares about me or my family. No one will protect me. My parents can't win against money. There is only one place I can go.

Dear Diary,

So I took a walk to Alice and Patrick's house. They welcomed me in, we had sweet tea and discussed memories of Arthur and Alice. I felt so at ease with them. They helped me take my mind of Bernard. I told them about my fears of him taking me. Told them that my parents would not be able to take him on with all the money he has. I begged Patrick to use his influence in this town to help them try to keep me here. To keep me safe. I had no idea of his plans. Well I didn't till Alice told me. She said he is planning on fixing this town up and taking me away to the City that is over twelve hours away from here, to a life of riches, more children and a happy marriage in a big house. I could not believe it. I begged them not to let it happen. I told them I only wanted to be married to Arthur, only wanted to be Alice's mum. Alice actually told me to stop being selfish. To enjoy what life was giving to me on a plate. Told me I had no say in it. A young attractive woman like me should be grateful I was chosen to lead such a lavish lifestyle. I don't want Bernard or his money. Tonight. Patrick and Alice told me I was no longer their concern.

Dear Diary,

Today Bernard came around again. Telling my parents that as soon as business is finished by the end of the week he is coming to claim me. My mum has said she will take me away. But we all know if that was to happen my father will pay the price with his life. I was not about to let that happen. I have no options. I have no choice. I am to leave my home once again. Only this time I am to leave with a vile man and travel over twelve hours away and never. Ever. See my family again! Bernard will make sure of that.

Dear Diary,

Today I met up with Mary, told her everything. She said she will talk to Ralph, see if he can do anything. He is now the town's lawyer. I am praying he can help me. I was in town with my mum and everyone was staring at me, whispering about me. I bet they all think me selfish for wanting to pass up such a life with Bernard. Have they all forgotten about Arthur? They all celebrated our wedding party with us. These were not my friends or my neighbours any more. All I had was my parents. I really did not want to drag them through all this.

Dear Diary,

So Ralph can't do anything to help me. Tomorrow afternoon, Bernard will be at my door and he will come to claim me. No one in this town that has money will help me. No one cares what might actually happen to me. They see me as the lucky one, leaving town to live in the life of the rich. My heart, my body, my soul belongs with my Arthur. I despise Bernard. He will never have my love.

Dear Diary,

Mum made an entire spread for tea. A variety of every food I ever loved. A farewell tea I guess. Bernard dropped a letter through the door. It said that tomorrow I am his. He will collect and payments will be made. I could barely stomach the sight of all the food after that. My mum and dad did all they could to take my mind off things. We laughed, dad joked. We reminisced about the good times in my childhood. We talked of Arthur and Alice but that made me cry. I helped mum clean up, then we played card games until we were all ready to sleep.

Dear Diary,

I slept in my parent's bed. None of us ready to say goodbye. None of us wanting too. Mum made breakfast, eggs and fine bacon. Very fine indeed. I know all this food would of cost a lot of money and probably set them back ALOT! A farewell breakfast I guess. Mum and dad have been taking my mind off things. We all have to the realisation there is nothing they can do.

Dear Diary,

After lunch a note came through the door. Inside it held a letter to my parents. Then a load of notes. A lot of money. More money than my parents have ever seen in their lives. We all just cried as we stared at the money. Mum said she will never accept it. Dad said he would burn it. Tonight Bernard will be coming to collect me. Tonight I will say goodbye to my parents and my home town for the last time. I will never see either again.

Dear Diary,

Two weeks ago, Bernard came for me. He ripped me from my mother's arms. The town looked on. He got someone to beat my dad up in our garden, through money at them and spat at them. Disgusting man. I saw all the faces of my neighbours as I was dragged towards a car. On the way out of town I spotted Alice and Patrick watching from their front gate, they turned and walked away as if I was no one. As if I was a nothing scumbag being taken to jail. I AM STILL MARRIED TO THEIR SON!!! they don't care. These last two weeks have been hell. Bernard brought to a six bedroom, 5 bathroom, two reception room mansion. Very refined. Bigger than the Hughes household. He is definitely richer. He showed me around the house. I was not impressed. He is vile and I will never want him. He showed me to my bedroom. Thank god we don't share one. He put my case on the bedroom floor. Told me to change and freshen up. A few hours later he came into my room. He sat on my bed and told me. Told me how my life will be from now on. He will come and take me when ever he wants, however he wants. He is going to marry me as soon as possible and I will have his child within the next year. Can you believe him? I will never give him my body.

Dear Diary,

Today Bernard dragged me to the local registry office and married me. Our witnesses were two of his security guards. It was dirty, fast and not a wedding I would wish on my worst enemy. When we got home he sent me to my room while he drank with his work men. Later he came in. completely drunk. The alcohol on his breath burnt my nostrils. He tried to touch me, kiss me, I kept pushing him away. He wouldn't stop. He wouldn't let me go. Tonight was the first night he took me. Hard, rough, quick. He was disgusting. I felt so ashamed. I cried after he left. I felt like I was nothing. I felt I had betrayed my Arthur.

Dear Diary,

The last few months have been hell. Bernard keeps me trapped in this house. I have access to whatever I want. But I don't want anything. I want my family. My Arthur. My Alice. My Bruno. He takes me when ever he wants. The last time he did it seems to have made me with child. Yes. I am having his child. I feel disgusting. How can I bond and love a child that belongs to him? I hate him. Will I hate this child?

Dear Diary,

Today the doctor told Bernard and I that the child came away from the womb. I am no longer pregnant. I cried for a long time when I was finally alone. I had that child inside me and came around to the idea of trying to give this child some of my love. Bernard was not happy. Once the doctor left he got drunk and accused me of purposely losing the child. He beat me. He never beat me before. The look in his eyes said he enjoyed it. Now I think I shall have that more as well.

Dear Diary,

Bernard has just left my room. He came in drunk. Felt like beating me. Called me a whore. Told me I killed his child. He took me in the most vilest way. Threatened me. Told me he did not want me to be pregnant again, said there was only one more place to put it. Yes. There. He forcefully entered me while beating me on the back and pulling my hair, calling me all sorts of horrible names. Blaming me for the baby. I cried. The whole time. I begged for it to be over. He took even longer this time. More drunk than usual. Enjoyed hurting me more than the act. He took so long. I felt physically sick when he finally stopped. He got up and left. Left me there in a state. Tears falling down my face, my back bruised, my hair on my bed, where he had pulled it out, my body sore and aching.

Dear Diary,

I don't get much time to write in this. It has been a few months since I have. I am with child again. Doctor reckons I have a few months left. I am getting bigger and bigger. Bernard no longer takes me, nor does he beat me. I have been left alone completely. He makes sure I eat and drink and attend my doctors appointments. He has however threatened me. Told me I really do want to have this baby live or my life won't be worth living. How wrong he is. My life already is not worth living. I don't want this baby to be brought into this world with him as a father. He is horrible. I do not love him. I hate him. I do not want this baby. Yes, I have no choice, it is on the way. But how will he treat it? Will he beat it if he is drunk? Will he love it?

Dear Diary,

Today I gave birth to a son. We named him Richard. Sadly he was stillborn. I am told I have to stay in hospital to rest. Bernard was furious. He wanted me home. No doubt to punish me for yet again not giving him a child. I really do not want to go home. I prefer the vile hospital food and the doctors rather than being alone with Bernard.

Dear Diary,

Today I am returning home to Bernard. Doctors say I am rested and well enough to go home. I really don't want to. I am so scared. I know I am going to feel his wrath as soon as I am back in my bedroom. The thought alone makes me cry, makes me feel sick and I am scared for my life.

Dear Diary,

Again Bernard has left. He beat me completely. Leaving no skin untouched. Every inch of me is bruised. He took me so many times I am really sore, both places. He was not gentle. He hurt me and enjoyed it. Called me a child killer. Told me I was a whore and I needed to forget about my past and give him a child. Said if I didn't give him a child soon he would kill me. Chills ran up and down my spine. I really do believe him. I know he will kill me. But it really is not my fault. I didn't know the first baby would come away from my womb or that Richard would not take his first breath. It is killing me that these children are not living. That I can't give them life. A life they deserve. I feel like I am to blame. The doctor said I need extreme rest. He said I might be able to carry and deliver a healthy baby if I had full bed rest and was at home in comfort during delivery. That doctor did not know what my home life was really like. Living in fear, being beaten daily, taken whenever the fancy takes your husband and being tortured. How can I relax? No he does not do these things during pregnancy but how can I relax when I am worrying over what sort of life the child will have?

Dear Diary,

Bernard came into my room before. Told me he was taking me away. Said I needed a break from this house. From the memories of our babies. Said we need to make our babies in a peaceful location. I am currently packing my bag.

Dear Diary,

I managed to sneak this diary in my case. We are at a motel. It is very fancy. We have a double bed, clothes storage and a radio. It is lovely. Tonight Bernard is planning on ordering some food and making a nice picnic on the bed. His idea of romantic.

Dear Diary,

Bernard took me tonight. It was gentle, it was slow, it was quick. He was not drunk. He kissed my neck and kissed my lips softly. I hated it. I knew he just wanted to get me pregnant. I could never give myself fully to him. I hate it. I don't want him. I never want to have his child. Never. I cannot wait to just get out of this slimey motel. I wish I could run away. But he would catch me and I would be punished. I know this. I tried you see. I waited until he was finished and had fallen asleep. I opened the front door as silently as I could. I managed to close it and I ran, I ran for the open road. I made it to the bottom of the stairs when I felt hands gripping my hair. He dragged me by my hair back to the motel room. No one batted an eye lid, we were just a couple having a disagreement. He slammed the door shut and threw me on the bed. He pulled my hair and took me in the place he knew I hated. When he was finished he locked the door. I felt sick and ashamed. He made me sleep on the floor with no blanket.

Dear Diary,

During the night he would come to the floor and take me. I would be awoken by him on top of me. After he was done he would go back to sleep. I barely slept. He kept coming back. Like an animal. He used and abused me and he loved every minute of it. He was sick. Today we go back home. He said I better be with child or I will pay. I can't believe it. He makes it sound like a romantic night away. It turned into hell. He hurt me. Tonight was no different than being at home. I can't relax enough to ever carry a child! Not with this monster!

Dear Diary,

I have had enough. Today I am planning my escape. I want out of this hell. This place, this monster. This life is not for me. I can't do it any more. I can't take any more of these beatings, the way he takes me, when he wants it and roughly. If I don't escape now I never will. I will die here. He will kill me if I can't make another child live. I know he will. He has threatened it. Trust me, he keeps his threats. My whole body aches, I am black and blue. I am worn out from the raping. I am not physically strong enough to carry another child. So today I am off. Leaving this hell and headed home.

Dear Diary,

He caught me! I got half way down the drive way and I felt a sharp pain in my foot, it happened after a loud bang. I fell to the floor immediately. Yes. He shot me. He came over to me, dragged me to my feet by my hair and thrown me over his shoulders. When he locked the front door he threw me over the couch, before I could hit the floor he held me over it. He took his belt and beat me with him. He then pressed himself into me. He pulled my hair and punched my back. Afterwards he took my foot, warmed it in water and healed the damage. Thankfully I won't lose it, just clipped my skin, enough to send me straight to the floor though. He took me to my bedroom. Beat me up again. Left me black and blue on the bedroom floor after he spat on me.

Dear Diary,

For the third time I am with child. Only just found out the news. Bernard has had me in bed ever since. Says I will get all the rest I need and has arranged for me to deliver the baby here should I go full term. He has made it pretty clear that I should go full term or else. To be honest there is nothing left for me. He can't do any more than he already has, beaten me down, taken my confidence, my freedom, my life from me. I will never want him. I will never love him and I will never fully give myself to him. He can take but I will never give. He disgusts me! I wish he would just die already.

Dear Diary,

Six months in to pregnancy. I sure am ready to leave this bed. All I have is toilet breaks to keep me moving. I am so fed up. Bernard makes sure I am awake for doctors to come to the house, the baby is growing fine, healthy and well. I am apparently blooming and I am in good health. Bernard never takes me. He never beats me. To be honest, when I am with child it is the only time I get peace from Bernard. Even though the child never lives, it is my only freedom from his fists. From his mental abuse and his horrific torture. A few more months and hopefully this baby will be born healthy and alive. I am seriously scared of losing another baby. This one might be my only chance.

Dear Diary,

Today I gave birth to a healthy baby boy. His name is Andrew. Bernard took him straight from my arms. He only lets me see him when he needs feeding or changing or burping. The rest of the time I am laying in bed alone, hearing the baby downstairs. I finally had a healthy baby born. But I am scared I will not be allowed in it's future much.

Dear Diary,

Andrew is nine months old now. He is very boisterous. I am his full time carer, I make sure he is fed, cleaned and in good health. Bernard takes him out to places, leaving me behind to do the house work, the cooking. He fired his cook and housekeeper when Andrew was born. I had to take that role on. I had to do everything and make sure both of them were well taken care of. To be honest I proffered my life cooped up in that bedroom. Andrew doesn't like me. Bernard makes him slap me while holding Andrew's hands. This makes Andrew giggle. He puts me down in front of our son and I am scared how Andrew will be with me as he gets older. Tonight after I put Andrew down to sleep, I must make sure I clean up all the toys, feed Bernard and make sure his room is tidy and the bed ready for him to just jump into it. Before he goes to bed I am sure he will creep into my room and beat me while he takes me. That still happens. Ever. Single. Night. He says he wants me to have at least one more child. I could not handle another child hating me as well.

Dear Diary,

Today Andrew turns one. His party food is all made and he is getting ready with his dad. The only people at this party will be me, Andrew and Bernard. Andrew is just like his dad. He kicks me, pulls my hair and tells me how much he hates me. His dad laughs and says that's my boy to him. I have to grin and bare things today. I am going to change and then be the perfect wife and mother.

Dear Diary,

Andrew hated the food. Like his dad he would moan at this and moan at that. The presents I handed him weren't wrapped good enough, but his dad could do no wrong. He is a horrible little boy. I never thought I would despise a child of mine. But I do. I really hate him. Like I really hate his dad. He hurts me, laughs in my face and never listens to me when I tell him what to do. All I could think of today was my Arthur, our life together. Remembering when we moved into the apartment, the day we decorated rooms and the day I received Bruno. Thinking of the good times makes me resent my life now even more. Thinking about my Alice. My lovely Alice. She was so beautiful, with her dark hair and bright eyes. She looked so different when she died. Pale, grey eyes, hair was thin and faded. She was so frail and ill. She was in a lot of pain. In a way I was glad when she got the release. But she left me behind. Her and her father left me behind. Now I am left with Andrew the child I hate, the child I never wanted and Bernard, the man I loathe, the man I will never love, will never give myself to. He can take me, beat me, but he will never break me. I am Maggie – Leigh Hughes. Wife of Private Arthur Hughes and mother to Alice Hughes. In my head my life is so different. Sometimes I daydream of a life I used to live. One filled with love, happiness, joy and a life I would give anything to have back. I used to work, pay my own bills, live in my little apartment with Alice and Bruno. I decorated it myself. Now I live in this massive dungeon. I live with fear of when my next beating will come, fear of my child, how he will be with me as he gets older. He is

violent with me now and he is only one years old. This is
my life now. For the rest of my life I am in this hell.

Dear Diary,

A few months have passed since I wrote in this. Bernard has taken Andrew out for the whole day. I am enjoying the peace and quiet. I was trying to dress Andrew and he grabbed my hand and bit me. Bernard laughed and told me to hurry and get him ready. I did as I was told. To be honest, I am feeling a little low today. This life I lead is not going away. I try and escape but he catches me, then he beats me and takes me as an when he wants. Andrew hates me and he is sometimes violent as well, he bites me, kicks me, tells me how much he hates me. His dad just laughs it off and says that's my boy. I'm so sick of this life. I feel like I want to just die now. I miss my parents. I want to see them so bad, but I know he won't take me back there. I am trapped here in this house, in this life, he disrespected my parents, the townspeople did nothing to save me so that they could have new buildings and a fancier town. Alice and Patrick turned on me. Told me I was not their responsibility any more. Arthur surely would turn in his grave at the way I have been treated. I wonder if he is looking down on me now, with our Alice. I wonder if they finally met each other in the after life. If heaven exists I am sure they are both there together, watching me from above. The thought is warming my heart. I miss them both so much. The life the three of us should have had still plays in my mind. The thoughts get me through the days. Knowing they are up there waiting for me gives me hope.

Dear Diary,

Tonight was no different that any other. Bernard came into my room, drunk. He took me whilst telling me how ugly I am, how much of a bad mother I was, how I disgusted him, how easy I was. How much he wished I was dead. After he finished before he left, he told me he wishes I would leave him and his son to enjoy their lives, said he wants me in a grave. Said no one would miss me. No one would ever know what happened to me. That sent chills down my spine. Is he planning to kill me?

Oh I hope he is…

Dear Diary,

Today is Andrew's first day of school. Private school. His dad can afford it. Standing before me in his newly brought and pressed uni form he is showing off to his dad. Bernard is beaming with pride. I could care less. I hate the child. Bernard has taken him. Of course, I am not allowed out of the house. I have to stay here and see to the chores. Every day Bernard makes a list for me of things to do, what to clean and what to cook for tea. He leaves said list pinned to the memo board. I hate him. Today I am feeling a little unwell. I am sniffily and cold, coughing on and off. I hope it is the flu, I hope I die, soon and fast, quick and painless. I want to be with my Arthur and my Alice. I want to live in peace. Well I best get on with the chores.

Dear Diary,

Bernard came back, gleaming. Telling me how proud of our son he was. We sat at the dining table while we had lunch. He did the usual, I should be more proud, show more emotion, be a proper mother. I am sick of his vile words. I don't want to love Andrew and I certainly am not proud of him. He is spoilt, unloving and a bully. Just like his father. I distance myself from the child. It is hard for me to comprehend having my beautiful Alice and that evil Andrew come from me. I hate him. Tonight I am expected to cook tea, bath Andrew and make sure Bernard gets plenty of alcohol. My life. I loathe my life.

Dear Diary,

A few years have passed since I wrote in this. I became ill with a flu that caused me to lie in bed all day. It messed with my brain and I had to learn to read and write. The last few years have been horrible being ill, but wonderful. Andrew and Bernard never bothered me. Bernard hired a house keeper and cook as well as a nanny. I spent every day and night in my bed. Never seeing that vile man. He never came near me, in case what I had was contagious. He always sent the doctor in alone. Andrew never came in this room anyway and Bernard never wanted to chance him catching anything. Bernard came up here before, told me Andrew is starting high school soon. I told him I am feeling much better now, my doctor and teacher will be around later. My doctor is discharging me as I am fully recovered. And my teacher is coming to sign me off the books as I have fully learnt everything. How to read and write. I can even remember things again. From my childhood and memories of my beloved Arthur and my darling Alice, even memories of my sweet Bruno, I remember my parents, my old friends. I even remember the dreaded day I was dragged here against my will and left to live in this hell.

Dear Diary,

Andrew is bringing a girlfriend around apparently. How grown up of him. Courting someone. Poor girl. I have to have tea ready for a certain time and be on my best behaviour Bernard has already warned me. Even Andrew got his moneys worth in. Told me he would leave me black and blue if I did anything to put her off him. I believed him too. He is now 6ft at the age of 16 and built strong. He has beaten me a few times. Saying his food wasn't good enough. His clothes weren't ironed to his standards. His dad laughed it off as usual and then that night made sure I would never do anything to upset Andrew again. To this day I haven't. His clothes are ironed neatly and I always reheat his food even if it is fresh out of the oven.

Dear Diary,

So today I met Rebecca. Andrew's girlfriend. She was so lovely, long blonde hair, green eyes. Very beautiful. What she saw in that demon boy I'll never know. The way she looked at him, she was besotted. I remember that feeling. The butterflies, the rapid heart beat, the sweaty palms. I always had them feelings every time I looked at Arthur. Things went really well. They all complimented the food, Andrew left with Rebecca and Bernard was pleased with my behaviour. I cleaned the dishes and gave Bernard his alcohol. I then came up here and changed into my pyjamas so I could write in this. I know no one will ever read this. Arthur gave it to me on my 18th birthday. Said to write down my memories and life experiences. So I am. Only they are the experiences and memories I was hoping for. I was hoping to live happily ever after with my Arthur, raising our Alice and loving our dog Bruno. Sometimes I wonder if Arthur had lived would we have had more children together? Maybe a son. John. A kind, gentle, loving boy. The double of his father, just like Alice. I would have liked to have got a female for Bruno and enjoyed puppies for the children. All children love puppies. Except Andrew. He would probably kill it. Sick boy he is. I sit here, writing in this when ever I can. Sometimes months or years go by without entries, I sit here longing for a life I will never have. A life I should give up on. But how can I give up on something when I was always told not to?

Dear Diary,

Today Andrew and Rebecca are getting married. Of course I am not allowed to attend the wedding or the after party. Not that I want to anyway. I hope she never lives the life I am forced to. Every time I have seen her, she has shown no signs of beatings, no signs of him dragging her down with his vile words. She seems just as much in love with him as she was the first day I saw her. I wonder why he is so loving to Rebecca yet not to me. The woman who brought him into this world. Well with Bernard as his father, what do I expect? Plus I have never really shown him a love a mother should. I can't. I just can't. I want to, sometimes I even try to, but he says horrible things or hurts me. Then I realise I will never feel anything but hatred towards these two men in my horrible life.

Dear Diary,

Andrew and Rebecca had their third child today. I have been looking after their eldest two children. Mark who is 8 and Mary who is 6. I adore them both. They are loving, kind, gentle. Definitely take after their mother. I see them often. I am a young Nana and I try to remember what is cool and what is not so that when they come round they have all the latest stuff to play with.

Bernard's drinking habits have taken their toll on him. He has shakes, he gets breathless and cannot do as much activity as he used to. I am counting down the days...

Dear Diary,

Rebecca came around today with baby Elsa. She was so beautiful. I just could not wait to hold her in my arms. Andrew was cruel. Told me I could not touch her, that she was his daughter and I was to keep my hands off. Poor Rebecca didn't understand why he was acting like this as he never did when the other two were born. I just made sure I did not cause a scene and played with Mark and Mary instead. It cut me deep. I want so badly to hold that baby girl. To kiss her forehead and have the familiar baby smell fill my nostrils. I was still maternal. Just not to Andrew.

I wonder if my Alice would have had children. Would she have had a boy or a girl? Both? I think they would have been beautiful, just like her. Arthur would have been so proud of his grand children.

I am proud of Mark and Mary. Both are so loving. Every time I hear Mary's name I think of my old friend. She tried to help me with Ralph. Nothing they could do. I wonder if they are still in Grindley Cove, how they all are, what their children look like. I miss my friends. Peggy, Delilah, Mary and Patty and I all grew up together from a young age. I miss them all so much. I wonder if they see my parents. Are my parents even alive. I wonder if my parents miss me as well?

Dear Diary,

I have taken a few months off from writing in this. I have had to look after Bernard. He has become ill. The alcohol abuse taking it's toll on his body. His lungs and kidneys are failing. Doctors have said he will die. I am trying to keep him as comfortable as possible. Not that he deserves it. But it is bringing back memories of when I looked after my darling Alice. He is thin, weak and frail. He is pale and his skin has aged. I am counting down the days until I am free from him. I won't tell anyone else that. With Andrew now living his own life, having his own family, after Bernard dies there is nothing keeping me here, in this dungeon of hell. I am free to go wherever I want, whenever I want and I sure as hell intend to. I am going home. To Grindley Cove. To see my friends and family. I will go and see Alice and Arthur in Fort Delamere and take them beautiful flowers. I will spend everyday with them, make up for all these years away from them. No one will know where I went. I will never tell Andrew nor let it slip to my grandchildren or Rebecca. I shall miss Rebecca and my grandchildren. But they are not my family. As awful as it sounds they aren't. They belong to Andrew and Bernard. I belong to Arthur and Alice.

Dear Diary,

I stayed with Bernard while he took his last breath. I even comforted Andrew. He actually came to me. Hugged me and cried in my arms. I felt nothing. The moment Bernard closed his eyes I felt my freedom. Andrew asked to take over the funeral plans and I gave them willingly, as he quite rightly pointed out, he knew what his dad wanted more than I did. Bernard and I never discussed that sort of thing. We never really discussed anything. I would use Andrew and the funeral plans as my escape. I would leave while everyone was at the funeral. Yes, I would slip away. Andrew never knew my home town and I don't think he would travel twelve hours to find me anyway. Yes. My plan is to sneak away into the distance during the funeral.

Dear Diary,

Andrew, Rebecca and the children came round tonight. Andrew told me of the funeral plans, how his dad will be cremated (I hope he burns in hell) and how there will be a small service at the small chapel in the town on the outskirts of the City. He told me what time it would be starting and finishing. I said I would make my own way there. Told him I wanted to mourn in peace. At first he was not going to allow it, wanting control of me. He is a vile man. Thankfully Rebecca managed to persuade him to let me travel there alone. She understood I would need to grieve alone and said she would need that time alone if anything happened to him as well. God bless her. Of course she has no idea like everyone else I am planning on leaving and never coming back.

Dear Diary,

Today is the day of Bernard's funeral. I have my cases packed and everything I need for the twelve hour journey on the bus back home to Grindley Cove. I am ready. All the cars for the guests will be arriving at their homes any moment now. The car arriving for me is a taxi from a firm, not related to the funeral cars thank god. I have given him instructions to the main bus depot.

I made it. I am writing in my diary while sat on the bus home. I have money in my pocket thanks to that vile man I used to live with. Enough money to return home and buy my parent's house from them and live there until I am ready to be with my Arthur and my Alice again.

These hours are going by faster than I thought they would. We are an hour outside of Grindley Cove right now! I am ready to go home, hug my parents and be rid of my past. Well the past twenty odd years anyway.

Dear Diary,

Well I made it home. What I found was not what I left behind. The house I once called home was run down. The drive way had weeds growing out of the gaps in the cement. The house needed painting and it looked empty. Dead inside. I remembered on the off chance where my parents left the spare key. It was still there! I let myself in. The house was just as I left it. Only my parents weren't there. It was empty, the paint coming off the walls, dust and cobwebs in every room. I finally came to realise my parents had died, by the look of the house many years ago. I will go to the local solicitor and see what is going on with this property and maybe use this money I have to buy it. Tonight I shall sleep. In my old room. For the first night in a long time, I will let sleep fully consume me, I will sleep without fear, I will sleep with my old teddy.

Dear Diary,

I have spent my morning cleaning this house. It has not done any good for my bones. I am not as young as I used to be. Soon I am heading to town, I want to know what is happening to this house and how I can go about buying it for myself.

Dear Diary,

The solicitor was Raplh. He is not retired yet. He was so
glad to see me. We caught up on the years we lost. He
said he would send Mary round later to see me. He aged
well. Of course his skin has seen better days but we aren't
as young as we all once were. Anyway we got talking about
the house. My parents actually left it to me in their will.
They prayed one day I would return and re claim the
house. Take back what was mine and restore it. They were
so right. Apparently my dad died a few years back from
the flu and my mum died a few weeks later, the doctor
could only put it down to a broken heart. I can see that.
They loved each other dearly, their love was strong like
mine and Arthur's. I came back home and began looking at
what work needed doing in the inside of the house. I
headed into town and grabbed everything I could think of
that I would need. I did it in one trip hoping to not
return for a while. I really want to just get on with this
house.

Mary came round. We hugged for a very very long time.
She filled me in on her life. She has four sons. All adults
and living in the City. She said it's just her, Raplh and
their cat. She told me how Leonard and Patty died in a car
accident while holidaying. Frank had passed away and since
then Delilah had become a recluse and refused to see
anyone. Peggy and William were both still alive, together
they have two daughters who both live in town. Apparently
after I was taken Peggy stuck to William's side and never
spoke of me or of our friendship and she never spoke to

any of our friends again. I told Mary of my hell. Of the children I lost. The beatings, the registry office wedding, the way Bernard would take me, the prison I was living in, the child Andrew that survived but turned into a mini version of his father. She held me while I cried. I cried years and years and years worth of feelings. I was never really allowed to cry and I would never dare to in front of the boys.

That part of my life is gone now. I am going to spend the next however long of my life working on this house and spending my days in heaven.

Dear Diary,

I am starting on the outside of the house. It is the first thing you see and it really is an eye sore. People passing would recognise me and we would chat casually, others who recognised me would stick their chin in the air and walk on by, others never recognised me.

Today I am de - weeding and painting the fences.

I am ready to transform this house.

After the outside is done I am taking the bus to Fort Delamere to visit my Darling Alice and my beloved Arthur.

Dear Diary,

When I arrived at the grave of my husband and daughter I could see it was not looked after. There were no flowers, the grave stone had ivy around it and it was dirty. I had another task at hand. I will also work on bringing this grave back to its glory as well.

I told them both how I was back to stay. How much I missed them and loved them so very much. I placed the flowers in the vase I purchased and used the water from the garden tap.

When I return again I am bringing my gardening tools. I need to rid the grave of ivy and de - weed this entire area.

Dear Diary,

I have finally finished the grave and the outside of the house. I have spent every day doing both. In the mornings I would see to the garden and then make the hour trip to the next town to visit Arthur and Alice and get the grave looking beautiful for them. It has slowly taken its toll on my own body. I am getting older and certain tasks are getting harder.

I am more determined to completely restore the inside of the house as well before I leave. I want to die in peace. Knowing that Arthur and Alice had a decent grave and that my parent's home was as it should be.

I do visit my parents grave. They are the opposite side of the church, both buried together. As they would have wanted to be. I leave them flowers and tell them of my life and how I am back to restore the house. I tell my parents, Arthur and Alice daily of how much progress I have made with my tasks. I smile at the knowledge that one day I will join them all.

Today I was thinking of Andrew. Of how his family are. The children will be a lot older now. I wonder how he is treating Rebecca. Is he still a loving husband and father or has he finally shown his true colours? He is nothing more than a bully. Just like his own father.

Dear Diary,

Mary and I have plans today. We are going into town. I need some groceries and more things for the house. So far I have the downstairs finished and I am working on the upstairs. After that is finished I am re- furnishing every room. New sofas, new beds, new utensils and accessories. I am even buying a TV! How modern. I am used to myself and a radio but Mary insisted that I get one. Said she would be lost without hers. Yesterday Peggy died. Mary said she has no intention of going to the funeral. Says Peggy cut her ties from her dearest friends too many years ago. I wonder how William is. Should I care?

Dear Diary,

I had a lovely time in town with Mary. We are not as young as we once were though! My body is hurting. My old bones could not take me as far or as fast as they used to. We reminisced some more. I felt such loss. I missed out on a life with my dearest friend. Out of all the girls Mary and I were always the closest. She was my best friend. We met in nursery. We had the same colour hair and from then decided we were best friends. We still have the same colour hair. Grey. Ha! We met the other girls in primary school and we all sort of clicked and started to hang around together. I still find it hard to believe how all the girls became so distant with each other. Mary said she never cared, had her family.

Mary said she always hoped that one day I would return. I cried in her arms for the thousandth time since I returned home a few years ago.

Since being home, I have become weaker as I have gotten older, I have finally finished the graves for Arthur and Alice and my parents. The outside of the house is completely finished. I finally painted it and I do try to keep on top of the weeds. My body hurts so much I have to have breaks and sometimes wait a few days to even get out there to make a start on them. I have ordered new furniture for downstairs and apparently the men who will be delivering it will also help me place it where I want it. I have some accessories and utensils coming in the post and I have seen a brand new TV in a shop window in town. The store man said he will bring it round for me later. I am ready to see all the new furnishings fill this house. My parents would be proud with all the hard work I have put into this place and at the graves.

Dear Diary,

Today my furniture for downstairs arrived. The men were so nice, they put it all exactly where I wanted it. They were patient with me and I even made them hot drinks in my new kettle. A kettle! I flick a switch and it boils water! It matches all my new kitchen accessories. Tonight Mary is coming around to see the house. She even offered to help me with the painting upstairs. I know she just wants to help, Mary is a lot healthier than I am. Years trapped in a house with no where to go has damaged my bones and I am slowly developing arthritis. I really want to spend however long I have left mobile on this house. I need to finish it before I leave this world.

I made a start on the painting upstairs after Mary had left. She came round and we drank tea at my dining table. We laughed, talked about the good times and even clinked cups over old friends.

I miss my Arthur more. I know I won't live forever and as much as I am keeping myself busy with the house I really am counting down the days until I can be with him and Alice again.

That time really cannot come quick enough. But I must finish this house!

Dear Diary,

The upstairs has finally been painted. I have put orders in for new furniture up here and even have someone coming out to modernise the bathroom. This house is so beautiful and when my time in here ends I do believe that it will make a young couple very happy if they are looking for somewhere small to start out.

Today I haven't done much. Sat in my chair. My bones are getting weaker. My strength gone. I am really glad the delivery men will be doing all the heavy stuff.

Arthur keeps entering my mind. I really do feel it is a sign. A sign he is waiting for me. A sign my time is nearly up.

I see my darling Alice, before she became ill. I see her long dark brown hair and those beautiful eyes. Bright and full of life. Full of love every time she would look at me. Yes, my time to be with them is coming close.

Dear Diary,

Today my new furniture arrived and just like the last delivery men they put the furniture exactly where I wanted it. They too were patient with me and I thanked with hot drinks. After the left Mary came round. Poor Raplh had passed away. She was beside herself. I comforted her, cried with her. Sadly I never knew the man Ralph turned into, but I grieved for the young gentleman I once knew. Once Mary left I tidied up the house and found the strength to do some weeding in the garden. I am planning on nipping into town to grab something for tea.

Dear Diary,

I have plans today to travel to Fort Delamere to see my parents and Arthur and Alice. I miss them all so much. I cannot wait to see them. I have been so busy with fixing up the house. It has taken me years to complete as my bones and my body have not been on my side.

Dear Diary,

Getting to and from the next town is very hard for me now. I don't think I have the strength to do it again. I am really hoping I can. I need to be with them. It is all I have of them. Tomorrow we bury Ralph. I promised Mary I would be there. He is being buried in Fort Delamere as well.

Dear Diary,

Today we buried Ralph. After the service I stayed on to be with Arthur and Alice and then went over to where my parents were buried. I know this is the last time I can come here. Today has wiped me out. I am exhausted. These days I fall asleep in my arm chair in the lounge.

I comforted Mary when she came round. We drank to Ralph and reminisced. I told her that he is back with his friends and family now. She said she will be with him soon.

Tomorrow is my birthday. I am turning 90 years old. I remember my 18th birthday, when I received this beautiful diary from the man I love. It is filled with a life of memories and experiences. Some are wonderful, others are horrible.

I have no plans for tomorrow. I am hoping to see Mary. She said she would pop round to give me a birthday gift and card.

For now I must sleep.

Dear Diary,

Mary came round this morning. In her hand she held a home made birthday cake. We took half a slice each and washed it down with tea. She handed me a gift bag that was attached to her wrist. Inside was a birthday card and a new hand made scarf. It was beautiful. With winter around the corner I was very happy to receive a scarf. Winters in this town can be extremely cold if they are anything like I remember them.

A young boy came to my door today. I never ever receive visitors unless it is Mary. He came to tell me some bad news. Mary had passed away. Dropped dead in her door way after leaving my house. Neighbours found her apparently, lying out cold on her door step. She was now with Ralph.

I plan on giving her a good send off. I will speak to her children tomorrow and hopefully they will let me attend the funeral.

Dear Diary,
I am heading over to Mary's house today. I know her
children will be there arranging funeral stuff and I really
would like to attend. They don't know me but I hope at
some point my name was mentioned.

So after speaking to her children, they let me attend. The
funeral is next week, she is being buried with Ralph. The
children knew all about me. Said Mary would tell them
stories of us growing up together when the children were
young. They said when they were older she told them what
had happened to me. They all confided that both Ralph and
Mary both wished I would come back safely. Ralph had
regrets for not being able to help me. They were my true
friends.

Dear Diary,

Today I bury my best friend Mary. The service takes place in two hours time. I am dressed all in black. My hair brushed. It is so fine and so grey, not a lot I can do with it any more. Old age.

The funeral was lovely. The children knew their mother very well. The service and the hymns were perfect. The whole day was just as she would want.

The journey back took an hour as usual. As I sat on the bus I kept thinking about who would arrange my funeral. All my friends and family were gone and I hoped that Andrew would never know.

I have been thinking about Andrew a lot. Thinking of how he is. What Mark and Mary are like now they are a lot older. What Elsa is doing. I wonder how tall they are, what they look like. I wonder if he is still with Rebecca and did they have any more children.

Andrew never to my knowledge came to look for me. I was relieved. I wanted to escape undetected. I wanted to leave them all behind in that part of my life. I wanted to come home. I am so glad that I did. I was reunited with Ralph for a short time and my dearest best friend Mary.

Dear Diary,

Today I have woken up in my chair again. This diary is always next to me on my side table. I am feeling so weak today. I have not left my chair. I am not hungry or thirsty. I just want to sit here in peace.

I have since eaten. Had a drink of tea and a wonder around the house. I hold on to everything I can reach for. My old bones struggling to keep me upright. I had to look around each and every room in this house.

When I returned home, I made sure the graves were taken care of, the house was restored inside and out. I look around all these rooms at the beautiful paints and wallpapers and accessories. I am so proud of myself. Mary loved what I had done with the place. I know my parents would love it.

Dear Diary,

Night time. Bed time for me is sitting in my chair with a nice cup of hot cocoa with my little diary. My bones have been hurting all day, I have had sharp pains in my chest. I struggled to breathe before. I was daydreaming of my Arthur, remembering how handsome he was, all the girls wanted my Arthur, but he asked me to dance with him. The other girls hated it. We got married and began a life in the City. He gave me my beautiful Bruno. He was our dog. He was more than a pet, he was family. It crushed me when poor Bruno had to be put to sleep. Arthur didn't know but he also gave me our beautiful daughter, Alice.

She was beautiful and the light of my life. She was his double. Long dark hair just like Arthur. She had bright blue eyes that glistened just like him too. When she became ill part of me died with her.

I still remember how she looked in those last moments. White, skeletal and weak.

I think about my parents. Remembering Doris and Larry. I still remember how they looked when I was a kid. Then I remember how devastated they looked the day I was taken. Growing up I was the double of my dad. Fair hair, brown eyes. I was small in height like my mother.

I miss them all so much!!

16376763R00077

Printed in Great Britain
by Amazon